Readers' praise for *Grandmother Five Baskets*:

". . . a lesson in self-awareness and self-pride for young readers of any culture."

LaDonna Harris, *President and Founder*
Americans for Indian Opportunity

"The Poarch Creek Indians are very proud to be a part of this heart-warming story and its tribute to the importance of family."

Eddie L. Tullis, *Tribal Chairman*
Poarch Band of Creek Indians

"Together, text and illustrations are a tribute to a unique modern American Indian people, the Poarch Creek Indians . . . a lovely evocation of their spirit."

J. Anthony Paredes, Ph.D.
Department of Anthropology
Florida State University

"This is truly the Indian way of education . . . spiritual enrichment through basic temporal function, mentored by an elder."

Jane L. Weeks, *Executive Director*
Alabama Indian Affairs Commission

Grandmother Five Baskets

Grandmother

Five Baskets

by Lisa Larrabee

Illustrated by Lori Sawyer

Harbinger House

Tucson

HARBINGER HOUSE INC.
Tucson, Arizona

© 1993 Lisa Larrabee
Illustrations copyright © 1993 Lori Sawyer
All rights reserved
Manufactured in the United States of America
∞ This book was printed on acid-free, archival-quality paper
Designed by Harrison Shaffer

10 9 8 7 6 5 4 3 2 1

Library of Congress Cataloging-in-Publication Data

Larrabee, Lisa, 1947–
    Grandmother Five Baskets / by Lisa Larrabee : illustrated by Lori
Sawyer.
        p.   cm.
    Summary: Anna, a young Creek Indian, must call upon her own
discipline and persistence in carrying out her assigned task of
producing five traditional baskets under the guidance of Grandmother
Five Baskets.
    ISBN 0-943173-90-6 (pbk.)
    ISBN 0-943173-86-8 (hc)
    1. Creek Indians—Juvenile fiction.   [1. Creek Indians—Fiction.
2. Indians of North America—Fiction.]   I. Sawyer, Lori, ill.
II. Title.
PZ7.L32355Gr   1993
[Fic]—dc20   93-10451

About the cover: *The calico print shown on the cover represents
a typical fabric used for traditional dress among the Poarch
Creek Indians (see p. 33).*

DEDICATION

for Jenny

L.L.

for Mom.

L.S.

"Now, Mama?" Lucy asks, holding the five pine straw baskets I made so many years ago.

"Now, Mama?" Lucy's question tugs at my memories as surely as her hand upon my arm. Given voice, it lingers between us. Yet, I know it is a question for my heart, not my mind. . . .

Yes, little one. We begin today," Grandmother Five Baskets had answered twenty years ago to my insistent questions.

I ran to gather her shawl and basket as she pulled herself from the rocking chair. Though nearly eighty, she moved gracefully as she stepped from the porch.

She told me what I should look for, as we walked along the rutted red road toward the stand of loblolly pine trees where she always collected the pine needles for her baskets.

"Anna, this is a good time to gather the pine straw, since there was a heavy rain several nights ago. The freshest straw will be lying on top of the old, and we need only to pick it up," she said.

As we entered the cool darkness, the sunlight filtered through the pine trees. The light showed ferns and flowers pressing up through layers of leaves and pine straw.

Grandmother Five Baskets was right. The freshest pine straw was easily seen, its bright shine standing out against the older, darker layers. I began to gather the pine straw.

Grandmother Five Baskets moved slowly through the woods, stopping now and again, each time calling me back to look at one plant or another, and telling me its name and use. My favorite was a small bed of spearmint. The smell of the leaves was sweet and clean when crushed between my fingers. Grandmother Five Baskets said she would use the leaves to make a tea to soothe upset stomachs or in a salve to cool irritated skin. The afternoon passed for a pleasant hour or so, until we had gathered enough pine straw for several baskets.

Our shadows showed the way, as we walked back to her house. While the sun began its nightly journey, Grandmother Five Baskets told me that to learn the lessons of the five baskets would require much from me.

"Little one, you will find yourself tested now that you have decided to learn these lessons. And you will be learning more than just basketmaking. What your lessons will be, I cannot say. Some lessons are special to the person doing the learning. You will share problems others before you have had, but one or two of the problems you will discover are yours alone. While I will help as much as I am able, you will be the one who must finally help yourself," she said.

As I walked home, happy to be old enough to begin the lessons of the five baskets, I did not consider her words important.

"What can be so hard about making baskets?" I muttered, kicking the dust in the road as I walked the half mile home. Happy in the realization the lessons had really begun, I broke into a fast run. Suddenly, I was jumping, jumping, jumping into the air, as if to fly.

Grandmother Five Baskets was not my actual grandmother. In fact, she was no one's grandmother, as she had never married nor had children. She was my great-aunt, my grandmother's sister. Her name was Sarah McGhee. Yet, in our small Creek Indian community of Hog Fork, Alabama, there were very few people old enough to remember her by any name but Grandmother Five Baskets.

Through the years, Grandmother Five Baskets was the one called when illness visited a family. She cooked, cleaned, and tended to the young ones. She brought order where disorder had been. She comforted the dying, and welcomed new life into the world with each birth she attended. She doctored with herbs when doctors were scarce and medicines expensive, and she doctored with no-nonsense words when that was needed, too.

As my mother said, "Granny has shoulders wide enough for the whole world to cry on."

Her name, Grandmother Five Baskets, was not earned for her helping ways. It was for her skill in basketmaking and the lessons of the five baskets. These were seen, by those not having studied with her, as simple lessons in basketmaking. Yet, as any woman who completed her baskets learned, the lessons were much more. It was with deep love and respect that these women called her Grandmother Five Baskets.

Of the lessons in basketmaking, not every girl in the community wanted to learn them nor finished once they had begun. Girls were most often 12 or 13 years old when they began to study with Grandmother Five Baskets. Yet, from time to time, women as old as 20 or more studied with her.

Listening to all the talk among my womenfolk from the time I was small made me eager for my chance to begin the lessons. Yet, it wasn't the stories I heard that made the lessons appear special. It was the way the girls changed when they had completed their five baskets. It was as if they gained a maturity or an inward serenity. I wasn't sure anyone else noticed, but I had. Whatever they received during those lessons, I wanted it, too. Now, in the summer of my twelfth year, my chance was finally here.

During the next few days, Grandmother Five Baskets showed me how to clean the pine straw we had collected in warm, soapy water. I learned to rinse it well, and dry it carefully on old window screens laid on rocks in the sun. The screens allowed air to circulate completely around the pine straw and keep it from molding. I found reasons every day to stop by her house and check on its progress. After several days of drying in the warm sun, the pine straw was pronounced ready to use by Grandmother Five Baskets.

"Little one, the most difficult part in basketmaking might seem to be in the beginning. You must gather the pine straw into small bundles, bend them, and bind them with straw. This can be

discouraging when you are just beginning. Too many tasks for small, unsteady fingers to think about. I have faith you will do well with practice. Watch closely as I show you how to begin your basket," she said. I watched her nimble fingers begin coiling the base of her basket. Within a few moments, a strong, flat base was ready for the sides to be added.

I gathered my first small bundle of straw and my needle with straw binder, and I began to coil and sew. I struggled to keep my coils even as I worked. My tongue pinched between my teeth was as hard to handle as the needle and pine straw between my fingers.

Finally, there stood a completed basket, a little lopsided, but mine. Though it was only a few hours since I had begun the basket, it felt like years. I was tired and very pleased with myself. I had made my first basket. I could see that basketmaking wasn't going to be very hard at all!

"You have done well for your first basket, little one. When you come again, we will go gather the materials for your second. Do not judge this first basket too harshly, for your skills will improve with each one you complete."

After gathering, cleaning, and drying the materials for the next basket, the pattern of our time together began to set. I would spend an hour or more after school with Grandmother Five Baskets working on my basket or helping her to gather plants such as bloodroot, yellowroot, and bear grass. The bloodroot and yellowroot were used as dyes. The outer covering of the bear grass would be peeled away, and the inner fibers used for binding the pine straw together when making baskets.

The second basket was made with greater ease than the first. It was slightly larger than the first and made so the first basket would slip into the second comfortably, as a child slips into its mother's lap.

Spring came late that year. When it arrived, the warmth of the sun brought forth all kinds of plants and animals growing in abundance. Often at night, I would hear the dogs barking at an armadillo digging in our yard, or a possum on its nightly travels searching for food. During the day, the piney woods were alive with birds. The mockingbirds, with their easily seen markings of white on their tails and wings, were often about in the woods. During that spring, I found myself busy helping Grandmother Five Baskets to gather, dry, and store the herbs and plants we collected. On our trips, we would search out mullein for headache, pennyroyal for keeping away the mosquitos, and horsemint for colds.

Soon, I began my third basket. The beginning struggle to get a good, tight, flat bottom was lessening. I could feel my fingers beginning to instinctively *know* the right way to begin. This basket would be larger than the first two. My newly gained skill allowed me to feel that I knew all there

was to be learned about basketmaking, so the challenge appeared gone. I began to find my interests wandering toward other activities.

Spring gave way to summer and I found it easy to put more time between each of my visits to Grandmother Five Baskets'. The garden at home, the ball games with my friends, and the hours spent in long talks with my best friend, Lena, filled the hot, humid days. Whenever I would finish with my chores of weeding and watering the garden or dusting and sweeping in the house, I would run along the road to Lena's house. Thumping up her front steps, two at a time, I would hear her mother call out from the cool darkness inside, "Come on in, Sugar."

Once I was inside, she would always say, "You girls have yourself something cool to drink before you go out in that hot sun." There was always something at Lena's to chase away the heat of the day.

Lena and I would gulp down a glass of lemonade or iced tea, smiling at each other over our glasses. Then, down on the table the glasses would go, and out the door we would run. Across the field and through the neighbor's pecan trees to the shade of the big, old live oaks by the creek. Sometimes we wore our swimsuits and would fly into the water from the bank, laughing and shouting at the coldness of the water. More often though, we were content to sit quietly on the shore and dangle our feet in the dark, tea-colored water flowing by. Our conversations that summer were most often about what we planned to do when we grew up.

"I will marry and live in town," Lena would begin.

"I will go to college, and maybe I won't marry at all," I would answer.

"Now, Anna, you know that's foolishness. You have so many boys hanging around," she would say.

"Oh, those guys are only friends. They just want

a good catcher for their ball games," would come my quick reply.

I really wasn't sure what I wanted to do, but ideas like mine were guaranteed to upset Lena. She was much more traditional in her dreams than I. We would play our game of my-dreams-versus-your-dreams during those lazy afternoons, arguing the fine points. Yet, like the stream we sat beside, we would always find our way to common ground. Children and home were important in our both our imaginings, though we might come from different directions to get there.

The days of summer passed into weeks, and then into a month. Soon, two months had gone by since I had been to visit Grandmother Five Baskets.

I began to wonder why I had ever wanted to begin the making of the baskets. Occasionally, my mother would mention that she had seen Granny. Yet, no question was ever raised as to why I was no longer spending time with her.

Fall arrived and I found myself busy with the getting-ready-for-school buying trips. The time away from Grandmother Five Baskets had now drifted into month after month. The time with her faded from my mind, as it filled with homework, clothes, and boys.

Before I had time to think about it, the months had passed into November and preparations for the annual Pow-Wow for our Tribe. My older sister, Ellen, was hard at work making her dress, beading her earrings, and fringing her shawl for the Senior Princess contest. She kept busy with rehearsals and practicing her dance for the contest. I was busy helping my mother, baking pies and cakes for our church booth at the Pow-Wow.

Pow-Wow is a time for tribal members, families, and friends to gather together every year to renew our heritage and family ties. Pow-Wows are held at different times of the year for different tribes. Sometimes the day chosen is to celebrate

a season or special day of the year, a day which may be of great religious or cultural importance to the tribe. Thanksgiving Day was chosen for our Tribe's Pow Wow because so many of our tribal members had moved away from the reservation to find work. Holding it on this day allowed many more of our people to return for the celebration. Because it is held on Thanksgiving Day, it also draws many people from the nearby towns and communities who come to share in the festivities with us. Getting ready for it means much work and keeps everyone busy with preparations for several weeks ahead of time.

For my family, this was to be a special year. My three brothers and four sisters would be home to cheer on Ellen in the Princess contest. Our house would be filled to overflowing in every available corner!

Thanksgiving Day dawned bright and sunny. I helped carry boxes and bags of the food we had

prepared to the waiting cars and trucks. Lastly, with special care, we added Ellen's dress for the Princess contest. When we arrived at the Pow-Wow grounds, it was already crowded with people. Everywhere you looked, there was a rainbow of colors from the bright decorations on the booths and the dancing attire of the different tribes.

During the early morning, I slipped away to watch the Grass Dancers as the Pow-Wow began. It is a great honor to be a Grass Dancer. During their dance they dance the grass on the ceremonial grounds down into a circle for the other dancers to follow. My Aunt Eunice had told me the way the grass dance began was that there was once a young boy who was lame and could not dance with the other men and boys. The young boy was very sad and his heart would hurt whenever the others would dance and he could not join in. The Great Spirit looked down upon the boy and gave him the grass dance to do, so that he could be a part of the celebration. That is why the grass dance is danced with a stumbling step, as if the dancer were lame.

About noon, it was time for the Senior Princess contest. The family gathered around the ceremonial mound in our own cheering section. Ellen looked beautiful in her calico dress with ribbon trim, the fringe on her shawl swinging in time to her steps as she danced the slow traditional dance steps she had been practicing these past weeks. As the dance finished, we clapped and cheered and whistled. Ellen looked only at the judges, but I knew she was glad we were there. The judges walked carefully among the contestants, looking and making notes. Then huddling to one side, they talked among themselves. I thought I would burst waiting for their decision. Finally, Ellen was announced the winner! Our little band exploded into whoops and hollering that could be heard in the next county. This was a very special day!

During the afternoon, I was free to walk among the booths with my friends sampling all the good things to eat. We ate Indian fry bread, crisp funnel

cakes with powdered sugar, and Indian roast corn dripping with butter. As the sun began to set, we cleared and cleaned our booth on the Pow-Wow grounds. The cars and trucks were packed for the trip home.

At home that evening, the adults gathered about the kitchen table. Laughing and talking, they discussed the day and teased Ellen about winning the Senior Princess contest. My uncle John told her she won only because she had the largest cheering section. During a pause in the conversation, my mother pulled me close to her side. She announced to the group, "Anna is learning to make her baskets with Grandmother Five Baskets."

As all eyes turned to me, I wanted to run and hide. Yet, my mother's arms held me tight.

My Aunt Eunice leaned forward and said, "Honey, that's terrific! How many have you made?"

"Almost three," I mumbled. I was so embarrassed I scraped one foot against the other, staring at the floor.

I looked up in time to see my aunts and sisters look at one another. Suddenly one, then another, and another began to chuckle and finally to laugh out loud. Soon they were laughing and telling stories of their lessons of the five baskets and of all the distractions they had faced when they were learning to make their baskets.

"How could they make fun of me?" I thought. I knew I had not worked as hard as I should have and was ashamed. Quickly, I pulled free of my mother's hold.

On the back steps in the chilly night air, I could hear them laughing and talking in the house. Finally, my mother appeared at the door. She stepped through and sat beside me on the step.

Turning, I leaned my head on her chest. "Oh, Mama, how could they laugh at me?" I asked.

"Anna, they are not laughing at you. They are helping you," she said.

"Mama, I don't think their laughing is helping me," I sniffed.

"Anna, do you remember when Grandmother Five Baskets told you that during your lessons you would learn more than just basketmaking? Well, she tells that to each and every person who studies with her. For it's true, you are learning more than just a skill. You are learning about yourself," she said gently.

"Honey, not everyone wants to learn basketmaking, and not everyone who begins the lessons finishes them. It takes discipline and determination to see a project through. It takes courage to go back and finish what you have started," she said.

Tipping my chin to look into my eyes, she said, "There are those who dig deep within themselves to finish what they start, and there are those who quit. Which of those will you be, Anna?"

She gave me a hug and rose to go back into the house. I sat on the steps in the cold for some time that evening, looking at the stars and thinking of what my mother had said.

The next day when all the relatives were visiting, I slipped out of the house and walked the red rutted road to Grandmother Five Baskets'. Knocking softly, I heard her say, "Come in."

"Ah! Little one, come in. Your basket has been waiting," she said as I slipped through the door.

I walked to the shelf, retrieved the materials and partly finished basket. She pulled herself from her chair and moved to the table. Sitting next to her as I worked on the basket, I felt her hand on my hair and her whisper in my ear, "Now we finish."

The third basket was completed quickly. It was soon time to gather materials for the fourth and fifth baskets. The fourth basket was to be the largest and have its own lid. It was the outer basket.

Grandmother Five Baskets sent me to the stand of pine trees. She told me to collect the freshly dropped pine straw, and also to gather the green needles still on the trees. While the brown straw was washed and drying, the green needles were laid to dry. They would be used for the final basket.

The fourth basket began easily and flowed together without a struggle on my part. Even the lid was simple to do. Then it was time for the last basket. This was to be a tiny basket, which would nest in all the others. It was made with the fresh pine needles, now dried to a soft green. This basket took only an afternoon for me to complete.

"Anna, as it is so close to Christmas, I would like you to leave your baskets here for a while. You can come collect them after Christmas is over. I know your mother has many chores she needs your help with, so come see me after the holidays," Grandmother Five Baskets said.

The Christmas holidays were fun with visiting relatives, good food, card games played late into the night by the adults, and children getting under foot at every turn.

The evening after everyone had left, I walked the rutted red road to Grandmother Five Baskets'. I knocked and upon entering saw the five baskets

arranged on the table where we had spent so many hours working and talking. She had made tea and set out tiny cakes.

"Come in, little one. Tonight we celebrate. You have finished a difficult task, and we must honor the worker and the work," she said as I moved toward the table.

I sat in my usual chair as we talked about the holidays. I told her who had visited, and what I had received for Christmas. Then, as the conversation began to slow, she asked, "Little one, which of your baskets speaks to your heart?"

I looked the baskets over carefully. There was the funny lopsided first basket I had made. It was like a small clown smiling at the world in its tipsy, tiny way.

There was the third basket. The one I had almost not finished. There was the pretty outer one with its lid. Yet, my eye was drawn to the last basket, small and pleasant with its soft green color. I picked it up.

"This one," I said, handing it to her.

"You have chosen well, little one. You have made more than just these simple baskets. With these lessons you have been learning how to create your life," she said as she turned toward the baskets.

"Little one, these three inner baskets represent life. Each of us is born, we live, and we die. This lopsided basket is you at birth, and as you struggled to walk and talk. You were often very funny with your first efforts. The second basket is your middle years, and the third is you at the end of your life."

She picked up the outer basket with the lid. "This one represents the outer you that everyone sees. It is pretty now, but as all beauty does, it will fade," she said.

Setting the basket down, she held up the small, soft green basket I had chosen. "Little one, this is the most important of all your baskets. This basket represents your soul, that part of yourself that guides the quality of the person you are always

becoming. It is the beauty that is carried within you. This beauty will never fade and only grows stronger with the years," she said. She set the baskets one within the other until all were in their homes.

Pulling me from my chair, she held me close. "You have done well, little one. You have learned more than just a skill, but have also won against the tests you placed before yourself. You enjoyed the enthusiasm when the project began, and found the strength to overcome the boredom to finish your baskets when the excitement wore thin. Remember that everything in life moves in circles. Always know that the lows will follow the highs, that boredom follows enthusiasm as surely as day follows night. With discipline and humor you can overcome the challenges in your life to accomplish whatever you choose to do."

Giving me a hug and putting the baskets in my hands, her last words to me were, "Little one, remember what you have learned you will someday

be asked to teach to another. I know you will do well for your people, your community, and yourself. Never fear any task you undertake with love."

Walking home under the clear, starlit sky, I held my baskets close. I knew that I had learned more than just basketmaking. I had learned that I could finish what I had begun, that I could find the strength in myself to rekindle my interest in a long-term endeavor and win against boredom when my enthusiasm for what I had started dwindled. Perhaps one day, I would be able to pass along these lessons to one of my own. . . .

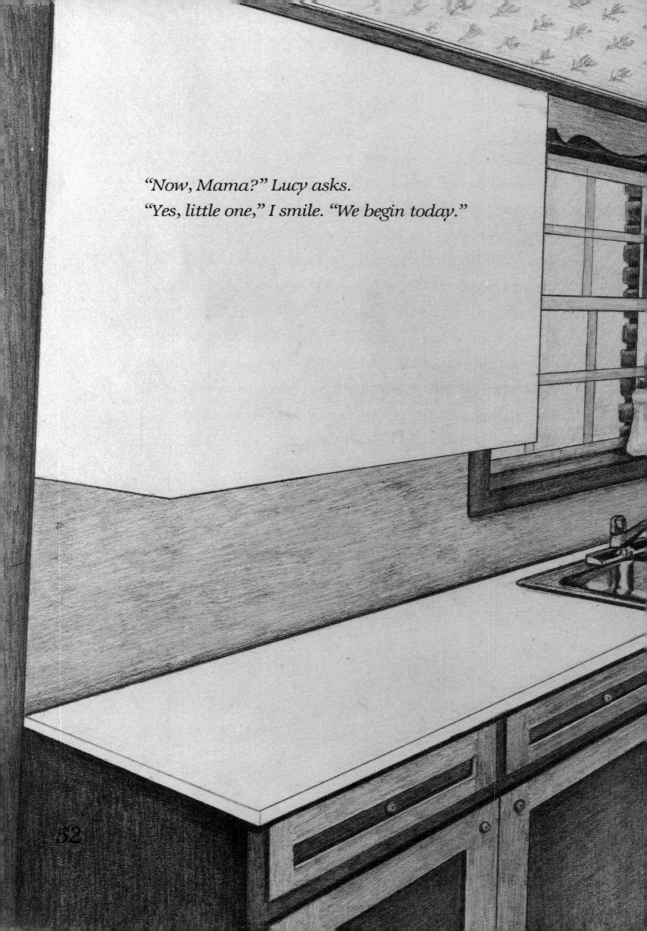

"Now, Mama?" Lucy asks.

"Yes, little one," I smile. "We begin today."

52

Acknowledgements

My thanks and gratitude to Rob for his unconditional love
and support; Gail and Tina Thrower for their help and
guidance in understanding the art of basketmaking; to Susan
Wicker, Robert Thrower, and William Bailey for their creative
direction in discussions of the Indian spirit; to Joe and Ellen
O'Barr, and Earl and Joyce Ann Jackson for welcoming me
into their hearts and homes; and to the Poarch Creek Indians
for giving me place and purpose.

L.L.

I want to thank my husband Tom, for helping me do the
work I love; my dad Glenn, for his support and suggestions;
Rachael, Tina, and Robert for their patience; Ray Pollock for
his kind patronage; and my family and friends for all their
encouragement. I appreciate my mom, Gail Thrower, for
teaching me to value family and tradition. I also thank God
for my daughter Sara, and all future generations, for giving
us a reason to learn, to share, and to keep tradition alive.

L.S.

Poarch Creek Indians

The Poarch Creek Indians are a segment of the original Creek Nation that avoided removal and has lived together for nearly 150 years. Despite the policy of removal of Southeastern Indians to Oklahoma, an indeterminate number of Creeks remained in Alabama.

The Creek Nation originally occupied a territory covering nearly all of Georgia and Alabama. The War of 1812 divided the Creek Nation between an Upper party hostile to the United States and a group of Upper and Lower Creeks friendly to the Government. The United States provided military assistance when hostilities erupted from 1813 to 1814. Upon victory of the Friendly Creek party and their federal allies, the Creek Nation reluctantly agreed to an enormous cession of land to the United States. The treaty compelled the Creek Nation to cede much of the territory of those friendly to the United States including the present site of Poarch. Those Creeks who had actively fought with the United States were permitted a land grant of one square mile.

Some Creek families, including the Gibsons, Manacs, Colberts, and Weatherfords, secured grants immediately after the treaty. Others, such as Semoice and Lynn McGhee, were

TENNESSEE

Memphis

65

Atlanta

Birmingham

ALABAMA

85

MISSISSIPPI

GEORGIA

Jackson

Montgomery

65

Poarch

Hog Fork

Tribal Complex

▲ Atmore

Mobile

Pensacola

10

FLORIDA

New Orleans

10

Tallahasse

Gulf of Mexico

N

The Poarch Band of Creek Indians

☐ Five-county tribal services area

▲ Tribal headquarters

0	50	100
miles

kilometers

0	50	100	150

unable to file their selections. In 1836, Congress passed an act allowing Lynn McGhee, and others to set aside 640 acres as reservations under the 1814 Treaty of Fort Jackson.

Today, there are nearly 2,090 members of the Poarch Creek Indians of which over 1,000 live in the vicinity of Poarch, Alabama. Poarch is eight miles northwest of Atmore, Alabama in rural Escambia County, and 57 miles east of Mobile.

Since the early 1900s, organized efforts have increased to improve the social and economic situation of the Poarch Creeks. Important educational gains were made in the 1940s. On August 11, 1984, these efforts culminated in the United States Government, Department of Interior, Bureau of Indian Affairs, acknowledging that the Poarch Band of Creek Indians exist as an "Indian Tribe." The Tribe is the only federally recognized tribe in the State of Alabama.

The Creek Indian Arts Council was established by the Tribe in 1988 to encourage participation and appreciation of the cultural, artistic, and historical resources of the Poarch Creek Indians and other American Indians.

The Poarch Creek Indians, in accordance with their Tribal Constitution, strive to assist tribal members in achieving their highest potential in education, physical and mental health, and economic development.

About the Author and Illustrator

When author **Lisa Larrabee** began a job in the tribal office of the Poarch Creek Tribe in Atmore, Alabama, she knew she had found the perfect setting for *Grandmother Five Baskets*, a multi-generational story she had been researching and nurturing for years.

Lori Sawyer's elegantly sensitive pencil drawings invite us into the dwellings of tribal members, and help us experience the scrunch and fragrance of the pine needles underfoot in the Hog Fork, Alabama woods. As a tribal member, and curator/educator of the Creek Indian Arts Council, she is uniquely qualified to illustrate the details of daily life of the Tribe. She diligently avoided blatant stereotypes of American Indians. There are no feathers or paint . . . these are moms, daughters, and grandmothers—basic relationships in all cultures.

Other Fine Quality Children's Books from Harbinger House

WALKER OF TIME
by Helen Hughes Vick

A compelling, fact-based mystery about a teenage Hopi Indian boy who "time travels" back to the final days of his ancestors in the cliff-dwellings of northern Arizona in A.D. 1250.

Ages 12 and up
ISBN 0-943173-80-9 $ 9.95 paperback
ISBN 0-943173-84-1 $15.95 hardcover

SON-OF-THUNDER
by Stig Holmås

An exciting novel of conflict and change, well-researched and set in the rugged Apache homeland in southern Arizona during the time of Cochise and Geronimo. A story for our times as we compete for resources in an ever-shrinking world.

Ages 12 and up
ISBN 0-943173-87-6 $10.95 paperback
ISBN 0-943173-88-4 $16.95 hardcover

OUTDOOR SURVIVAL HANDBOOK FOR KIDS
by Willy Whitefeather

From treating a bee sting to building an overnight shelter, this practical, easy-to-follow handbook gives children the knowledge and confidence they need to survive outdoors.

All Ages
ISBN 0-943173-47-7 $9.95 paperback

A KIDS' GUIDE TO BUILDING FORTS
by Tom Birdseye; illustrated by Bill Klein

From a blanket over the dining room table to dome forts, igloos, lean-tos, and a dozen more in all climates and environments, this hand-lettered, illustrated guide shows kids how to create their own secret places.

Ages 8–14
ISBN 0-943173-69-8 $8.95 paperback

LIZARDS ON THE WALL
by Ken and Debby Buchanan

With delightful verse and superb artwork, adults and children alike are brought to share in the wonder, complexity, and beauty of these charming desert creatures.

Ages 4–9
ISBN 0-943173-77-9 $12.95 hardcover

Available now at your favorite bookstore

or

Order toll-free 1-800-759-9945

Harbinger House
Books of Integrity
TUCSON